W9-DGF-557

Red Kite, Blue Kite

Ji-li Jiang

ILLUSTRATED BY

Greg Ruth

Disney • Hyperion Books

New York

First Edition
10 9 8 7 6 5 4 3 2 1
F850-6835-5-12288
Printed in Singapore

This book is set in Apolline Regular.
Designed by Abby Kuperstock

Library of Congress Cataloging-in-Publication Data

Jiang, Ji-li.
Red kite, blue kite / by Ji-li Jiang ; illustrated by Greg Ruth.—1st ed.
p. cm.
Summary: When Tai Shan and his father, Baba, are separated during China's Cultural Revolution,
they are able to stay close by greeting one another every day with flying kites until Baba, like the kites,
is free. Includes historical note.
ISBN 978-1-4231-2753-6
[1. Fathers and sons—Fiction. 2. Kites—Fiction. 3. Communism—Fiction. 4. China—History—Cultural
Revolution, 1966–1976—Fiction.] I. Ruth, Greg, ill. II. Title.
PZ7.J57396Red 2013
[E]—dc23 2012010000

Reinforced binding
Visit www.disneyhyperionbooks.com

To Baba and Mama, who experienced similar tragedy during that dark time, but survived with great courage
—J.J.

To my two boys, Emmett and Nate, who remind me each and every day of the irrepressible power of love and hope in difficult times
—G.R.

I love to fly kites. But not from the ground. My city is crowded, and the streets are skinny. Baba and I fly our kites from the tippy-top of our triangle roof. We are above but still under, neither here nor there. We are free, like the kites.

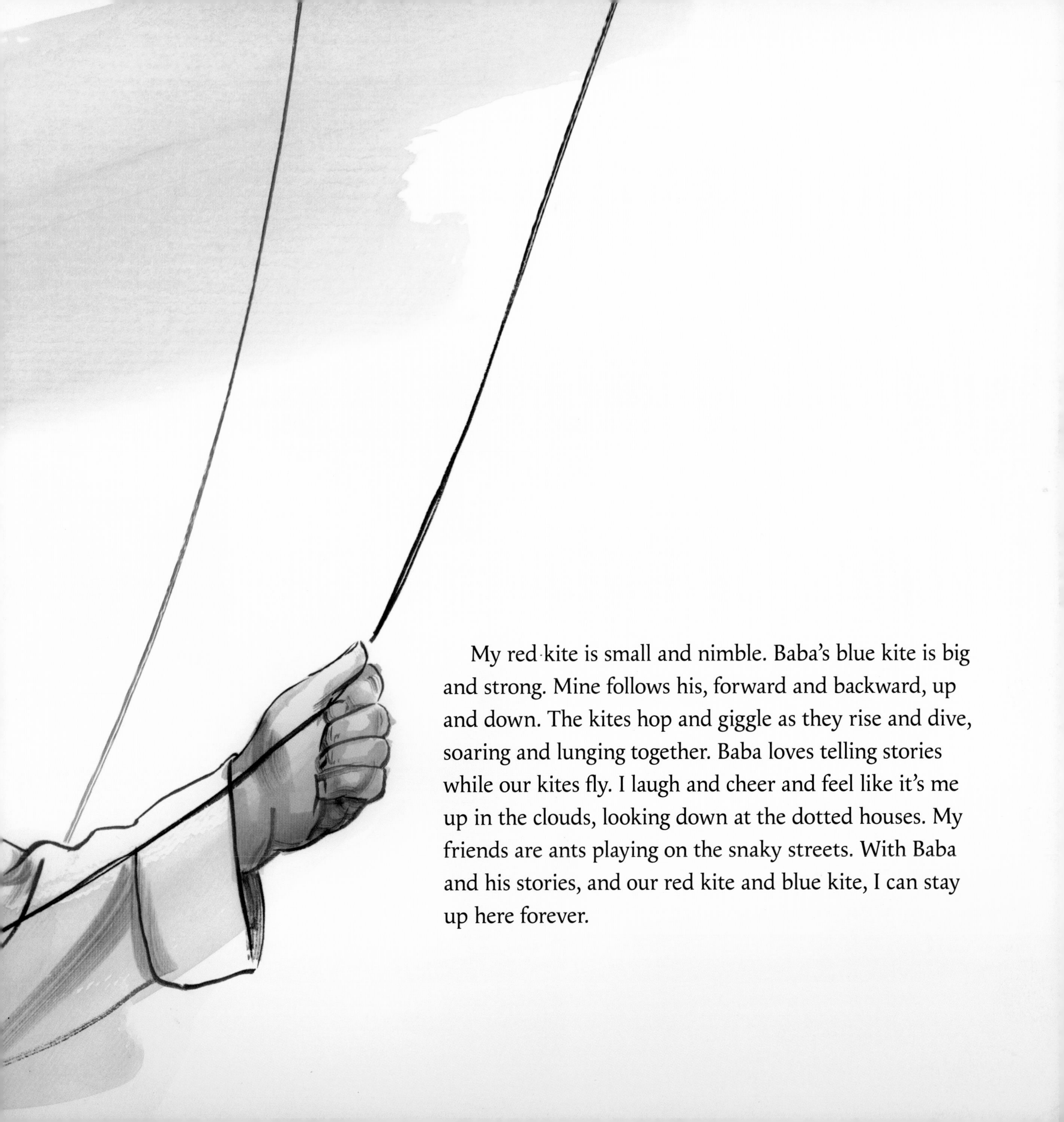

My red kite is small and nimble. Baba's blue kite is big and strong. Mine follows his, forward and backward, up and down. The kites hop and giggle as they rise and dive, soaring and lunging together. Baba loves telling stories while our kites fly. I laugh and cheer and feel like it's me up in the clouds, looking down at the dotted houses. My friends are ants playing on the snaky streets. With Baba and his stories, and our red kite and blue kite, I can stay up here forever.

Then, a bad time comes. My school is shut down. Soon all the schools are shut down. People wearing red armbands smash store signs and search houses. Men and women are sent to labor camps to work.

Baba is one of them.

Mama died when I was born, so I am sent to a small village next to Baba's labor camp to live with a farmer, Granny Wang. A thick forest stands between Baba and me.

Granny Wang lets me ride her buffalo, teaches me to braid a straw grasshopper, and shows me how to spin cotton on her wheel.

But at night my dreams take me back home, to the tippy-top of our triangle roof, with Baba and our red kite and blue kite. Above but still under, neither here nor there. Free, like the kites.

Baba visits every Sunday. He walks many hours from his camp just to see me. He picks me up and swirls me around and around until I become a kite.

Baba makes me so proud in front of my friends. He tells stories, shows us magic tricks, and arm-wrestles with us. But my happiest time is when we climb up the hill to fly our kites. My red kite follows Baba's blue kite, forward and backward, up and down. The kites hop and giggle as they rise and dive, soaring and lunging together.

When it's time for him to go, I walk with him all the way to the end of our village, holding his hand tighter and tighter.

"Fly your kite and be good, Tai Shan." He hugs me. "I'll see you next Sunday."

One Sunday in autumn, Baba comes without his smile.

"I'll be very busy and can't come to visit you for a while." He lets me sit on his lap and looks into my eyes. "But I have an idea." He takes out two big new kites, one red and one blue. "Every morning you can go to the hill to fly your red kite. I will see it from my camp. Every sunset I will fly my blue kite, so you can see it from here. That way we can see each other every day."

"A secret signal!" I shout.

The next morning, I get up early and run to the hill. I send my kite as high as it can go. The red dot nods and greets: "Hello, Baba. This is Tai Shan." I know Baba is smiling as he watches my red kite dancing.

Before sunset, I go back to the hill and climb the elm tree. I wait and wait. Finally, Baba's blue kite sways into the white clouds. The kite waves at me and whispers, "Here I am, my son."

Every day, Baba and I "talk" with our kites. My red kite soars and dips, shouting over the thick forest, "How are you, Baba? I miss you."

Baba's blue kite swirls and circles, replying, "I miss you, too, little Tai Shan."

How I wish Baba could fly like a kite and come here to see me.

Autumn is almost over. Leaves fall one by one from the trees, but Baba hasn't come.

One day, Baba's kite doesn't appear. The next day, there is no blue kite still. When I don't see it on the third day, I run to Granny Wang. "Please take me to see Baba. Please, Granny."

Granny hugs me and wipes my tears. "Let's wait one more day. If we don't see it tomorrow, we will go," she promises.

I go to sleep and dream again and again about the thick forest. Then I hear Baba whisper, “Tai Shan, I saw your red kite fly so high.”

Baba's deep voice instantly wakes me up. It is not a dream. Baba really is here with me.

I hug him tightly. "I watched your blue kite, too, Baba. Every day."

Outside I hear people coming. Baba puts his blue kite in my hand. "Tai Shan," he says hurriedly, "I will not be able to fly my kite for a while. But you can fly it for me. When you fly our kites, know that I am looking at the same sky and thinking about you."

The door flies open, and several men with red armbands rush in. When they take Baba with them, I try to run after him. But Granny grabs me so tightly that I can't move.

"Stay with Granny," Baba calls out. "Wait for me, Tai Shan. I will come back."

Baba disappears into the dark. I scream and kick. “Why did they take Baba away? Where did they go?”

“They are sending him to another labor camp. Very far. Only because they don’t agree with his ideas.” Granny Wang strokes my back and whispers, “He couldn’t fly his kite for three days because they locked him up. But he escaped and ran all the way here. He wanted to see you before he left. He had to.”

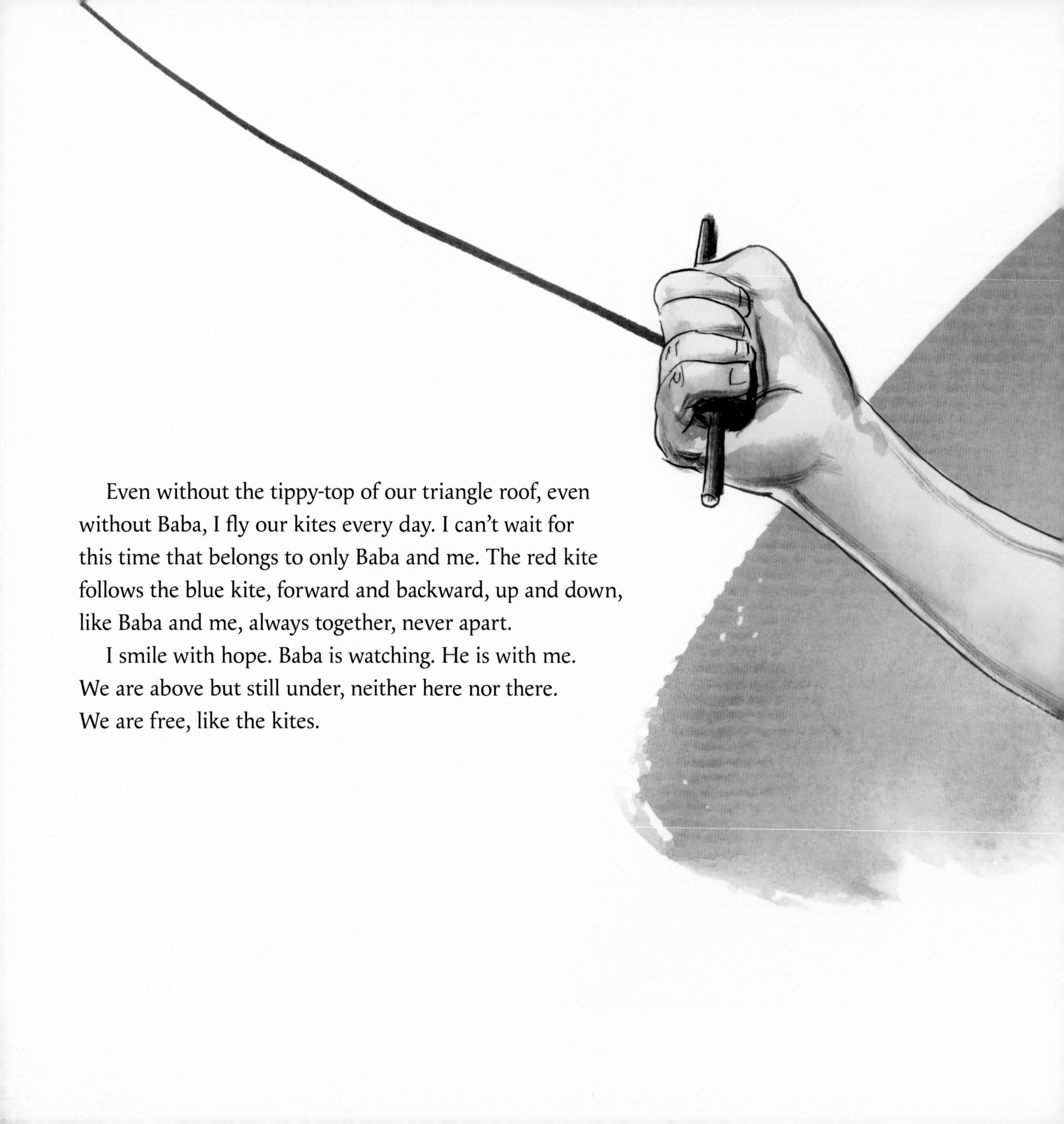

Even without the tippy-top of our triangle roof, even without Baba, I fly our kites every day. I can't wait for this time that belongs to only Baba and me. The red kite follows the blue kite, forward and backward, up and down, like Baba and me, always together, never apart.

I smile with hope. Baba is watching. He is with me. We are above but still under, neither here nor there. We are free, like the kites.

One bright summer afternoon, I let my red kite float among the clouds as I doze off on the grass. When I open my eyes, dozens of kites—red and blue—are waving and giggling at me.

I jump up and turn. Baba is standing there—thin and tired, with dark whiskers now on his cheeks. He is smiling at me, holding the string of a huge blue kite dancing in the sky. All around him, my village friends are smiling at me, flying their new kites.

"Baba—!" I run toward him.

"Tai Shan—!" He runs toward me.

The sky above us is filled with kites—red and blue. They hop and giggle and cheer as they rise and dive, soaring and lunging together. They are free, flying everywhere.

Author's Note

Whenever I see a kite flying in the sky, I remember the story of my family friend. When he was a little boy, he had to follow his father to a labor farm during a terrible time in China called the Cultural Revolution.

Between 1966 and 1976, the leader of the country, Mao Zedong, ordered all citizens to condemn and eliminate anything that did not meet the "revolutionary standard" so that China would not stray from the Communist path. People went crazy. Temples were destroyed. Classes were halted. Teachers and principals were beaten in front of their students. Houses were ransacked and personal belongings confiscated. Millions of people were labeled enemies of the country and then humiliated, tortured, and even killed. It was the darkest time in modern Chinese history.

My friend's father survived the Cultural Revolution, and my friend grew up and became a poet. This story was inspired by his experience. I wrote it for the many fathers and sons who suffered during that turmoil. Despite the darkness that kept them apart, their kites always flew, and their love never stopped.

—Ji-li Jiang